BUDDY
DOG OF THE SMOKY MOUNTAINS

Sincerely,
Bill Landry

STORY BY BILL LANDRY
WRITTEN BY RYAN WEBB AND SHARON POOLE
ILLUSTRATED BY RYAN WEBB

Celtic Cat Publishing
Knoxville, Tennessee

For Mom,
a friend to all creatures great and small.

-Ryan

Celtic Cat Publishing
2654 Wild Fern Lane
Knoxville, TN 37931
celticcatpublishing.net
celticcatpublishing.com

Manufactured in the United States of America
Book design and production by Ryan Webb

ISBN: 978-0-9847836-3-2
Library of Congress Control Number: 2013935007

Hi, my name is Buddy.

I am lucky to live in one of the most beautiful places on Earth, the Great Smoky Mountains.

I live with my dad Bill,
my brother Moxie,
and my sister Cali.

Bill likes to talk a lot.

We all live together
in a little cabin
on top of
a hill.

This is where I sleep
and keep my most
prized possessions.

I wake up early every morning.
Then I do the nicest thing. I help everybody
else wake up. I don't know why,
but my family never seems grateful.

After lots of coffee and lots of
bacon, Bill is ready to go.
He grabs my leash
and we head
out the door.

We walk down the hill towards
the Great Smoky Mountains.
Well, Bill usually walks.

I usually run.

Sometimes, when Bill is not looking, I go out on my own.

I say hello
to the trees
and the birds.

I say hello to the squirrels.

I say hello to the bees
and the butterflies
and the wildflowers.

I say hello
to the hikers.
They are always
nice to me.

Sometimes they let
me hike with them.

We stop to rest and eat. One of the hikers feeds me part of his peanut butter and jelly sandwich.

Later, I notice the sun beginning to set. It's time to head home.

I say goodbye and run
back down the trail.

I can run really fast but I can't read very well.

The moon is just a sliver tonight. The woods are very dark.

Oh no!
I think I'm lost.

Good thing I am not afraid of bears; only those pesky little chipmunks.

I run away from the chipmunk
but now I don't know where
I'm going. I am scared
and I feel so alone.

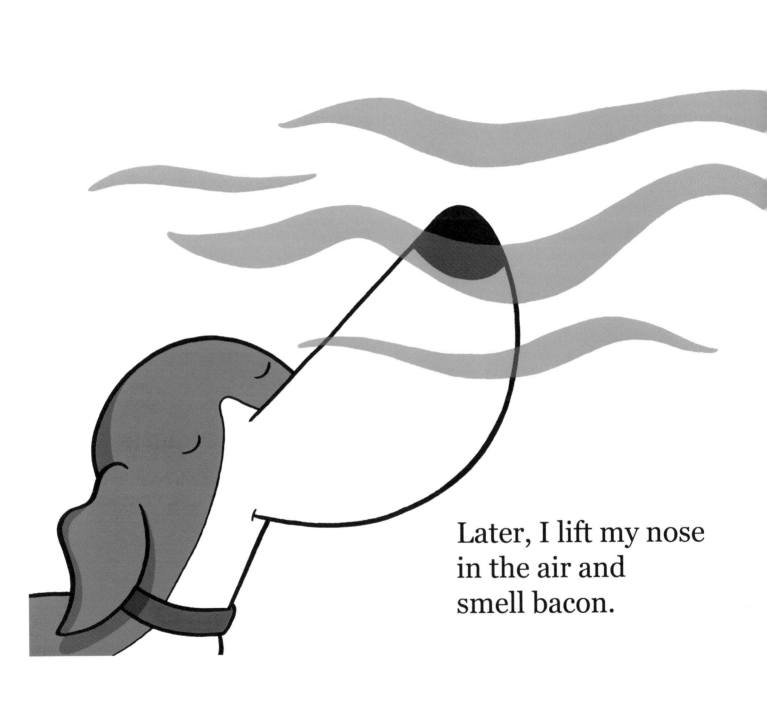

Later, I lift my nose in the air and smell bacon.

I rush towards the smell and see my home and Bill.

After some bacon
and a nap, I'm ready
for another adventure.

CPSIA information can be obtained
at www.ICGtesting.com
Printed in the USA
LVIW02n1004261213
366921LV00002B/47